KNIT TOGETHER
-A Novelette-
VIVIAN KAY

I0456725

E-Book ISBN 978-0-9950361-0-9
Paperback ISBN: 978-0-9950361-6-1
Ayoka Books, Ontario, Canada.

ABOUT THE AUTHOR

Vivian Kay is a Christian fiction author whose faith stories are woven around the themes of human imperfection, redemption and transformation. When she's not writing or daydreaming about writing, you'll find her playing simultaneous games of online Scrabble or snuggling up with a good book. Kay's debut novel, *Secret Places*, was first published by Brown Girls Books (USA) in November 2015. A wife and mother, Kay lives in a quiet corner of Canada's banana belt.

DEDICATION

To Jehovah Hoseenu, The Lord, Our Maker.
For you created my inmost being;
you knit me together in my mother's womb.
Psalm 139:13

ACKNOWLEDGEMENTS

First thanks to my Lord Jesus Christ for the gifts of life and inspiration. Every story I write takes me on a heart journey. I remain grateful for His grace and faithfulness.

Sincere thanks to family and friends, near and far, who support my dreams through prayers and encouragement. I appreciate every one of you.

To Oluwafikunmi Kilanko, Oyindamola Orekoya, Abimbola Dare, Unoma Nwankwor, Barbara Joe Williams and Michelle Stimpson, thanks for your invaluable critique and support.

My final thanks goes to all my readers around the world. Thank you for buying and sharing my stories. It's a great honour.

CHAPTER ONE

March 2015. New York City.

Marigold Shadd woke up to loud beeps from her cell phone alarm. Even though she was reluctant to leave the warmth of her bed, she had somewhere important to be. There would be plenty of time to catch up on lost sleep after she'd disembarked from the ship.

She turned off the cell phone, parted the nautical themed curtains on the lower bunk, and swung socked feet onto the worn blue carpet. The dim light from the table lamp her cabin mate, Buyisiwe, had left on guided her towards the bathroom door.

During Marigold's first work contract on a cruise ship, she'd walked into a closet-sized crew cabin whose thin walls vibrated the hum of the ship's engines and wondered how she and a stranger from Colombia would spend eight months in such close quarters.

Each year brought a new work contract, a different ship, and a cabin mate from another part of the world. It was like working for the United Nations on a minimum wage pay.

There were some squabbles over clutter and personal items being moved without permission. But, for the most part, she'd been blessed with awesome cabin mates.

In the bathroom, Marigold covered a yawn as she listened to Buyisiwe's loud snores. Most of Buyisiwe's time in the cabin was spent staring at the picture of her teenage daughter, a beauty with an impressive afro. The young lady attended a private school in their home country of South Africa thanks to her mother's ninety-hour work week sacrifice.

After she'd brushed her teeth, Marigold changed into a pair of jeans and a T-shirt and rubbed some shea butter lotion on her washed face and exposed arms. When dry, her hazelnut-coloured skin took on a hated ashy tone.

Marigold stepped out of the cabin and took the elevator to the fifteenth deck. The ship's corridors were empty of passengers. The wild "Last Night of the Cruise" party was hard to recover from.

She pushed open the swinging door of the main dining room, walked in, and exchanged a silent nod with the breakfast server sorting through a large bin of cutlery.

Marigold stood in front of the dining room's floor-to-ceiling windows and placed her hand on the cool glass. Situated near the ship's bow, the room offered the perfect spot for her to watch their vessel glide towards the New York Harbor. The imposing figure of Lady Liberty welcomed her from the distance. It really was the end of her decade at sea.

"Good morning, Mari."

She turned at the sound of the voice and watched as her best friend, Logan van Basten, strolled across the room. Long-limbed, Logan moved through spaces as if he had all the time in the world. Walking with him forced her to take slower steps.

"Are you all packed?" Logan asked when he reached her side. At five-feet-ten, she still had to tilt her head to look at him.

Marigold sucked in her cheeks as she nodded. They'd been together for an entire decade. During year five, they'd agreed that whenever either of them said it was time to return to Canada, they would both hand in their resignations.

Logan was ready for a wife, a couple of kids, and a thirty-year mortgage on a fixer-upper condo. In spite of many sleepless nights, she didn't know what she was ready for. For now, she would go wherever Logan went.

He reached out and held her hand. "We're going to be fine."

The way Logan stressed each word brought Marigold a sense of calmness. He'd always been good to her. Back in high school, Logan had asked her to be his girlfriend. Caught up in her grief, she'd said no. By the time they'd settled into their nomadic lifestyle and she was open to a relationship, it was clear that he had moved on. They became family. She couldn't ask for a better brother.

"We're going to be fine," Logan repeated as she continued to stare at his freckled face.

She tightened the grip on his hand. "I hope so Logi. I really do."

CHAPTER TWO

March, 2016. Toronto.

Head cocked to the side, Marigold stared at the A-Frame sign her colleague, Ziva, had placed on the sidewalk in front of their office. Location wise, their boss, Ayesha, couldn't have picked a better downtown address for the travel agency.

Ziva gave her an inquiring look. "What do you think?"

The bright blue, white, and red colours of the "Vive la France" slogan stamped at the top of the A-Frame sign was meant to catch the attention of potential clients. It was the agency's European getaway month, and France was the country of the day.

"Perfect spot. I hope it sells us more packages before Ayesha gets back from her trip."

Their agency specialized in curated travel experiences offered through customized itineraries. Because Ayesha wanted to sell more Asian adventures, she'd signed herself up for a Himalayan tour. Clients no longer wanted to shuffle stacks of brochures to find ideal getaways. They wanted firsthand accounts, pictures, and videos from a local's point of view.

"From your mouth to God's ears," Ziva said.

Marigold snickered. "Given the unending wars and natural disasters, I don't think He would be like hold the prayers regular church folks, I need to listen to these two travel agents who are looking to get paid."

Ziva chuckled. "Blame it on my Jewish mother. It's her go-to response."

She could relate. "My grandmother's go-to is: If it is God's will."

Ziva pursed her lips. "Baseless sentiments. We liberated heifers know better."

Marigold's faith took a nosedive after her parent's plane crashed into the Pacific Ocean months after her thirteenth birthday. The plane was still missing. Her parents and their friends were on a church mission trip to Ecuador. Since they were serving Him, God should have kept them safe.

Troubled by her thoughts, she changed the subject. "We should go in before we miss an important call."

Ziva gave the A-Frame sign another look. "You're right."

They walked into the agency office. Logan was still seated at his desk. Marigold could always tell when he had his wife, Alena, on the phone. His voice deepened and gained a sing-song quality. It was as if he was trying to lull the woman to sleep.

Marigold picked up the empty coffee mug on her desk and walked towards the small office kitchenette.

It had been just over a year since their cruise ship careers ended. For the most part, life had been good. Within a month of their return to Canada, they'd started the full-time jobs at the agency. It was where Logan met his Alena.

Marigold stood in front of the sink, placed her mug inside, and turned on the tap.

Fresh out of esthetician school, Alena and her three preppy friends had walked in and announced that they were looking for an adventurous trip. After Alena mentioned family ties to Iceland, Logan sold them a seven-day glacier and volcanic spring package.

Days after her return from Iceland, Alena visited the agency and brought Logan a bottle of Brennivín and a hand knit, wool sweater. Smitten, he'd asked her out on a date.

That first date led to several others. Logan went from saying to her, "Mari, I really like this girl," to "I've fallen in love with Alena."

Five months later, he splurged on a five-carat princess cut, diamond ring and proposed. Alena said, "Yes." Since they couldn't wait to live together, they chose a winter wedding date.

Marigold had stuffed down her feelings and done what a best friend should do. She got fitted for a female tuxedo and handled her best pal duties. The bride and the ceremony were beautiful.

Her stomach growled as she placed the washed mug in the dish rack. It was time to get some food.

"Sorry for keeping you," Logan said when she returned to her desk

"Lunch's on you." She turned to Ziva. "Do you need us to bring you some food?"

Ziva shook her head. "Just come back on time. I'm using my lunch hour for a hair appointment."

Marigold picked up her purse from the desk. "Will do."

With hands in his pants pockets, Logan was silent during their short walk to the neon green, food truck down the road. His silence unnerved her.

Lunch was a hot Italian sausage served on a bed of sautéed red onions on a toasted pretzel bun. She carried the food while Logan took care of the utensils and napkins.

Marigold found an empty picnic table at the nearby mini playground. Even though there was a little bit of snow on the ground, the warm weather heralded the arrival of spring. She waited until Logan had swallowed his food. "What's going on with you? You look like someone died."

Logan sighed. "Not someone. A dream."

"What do you mean?"

"Alena has Mayer-Rokitansky-Küster-Hauser syndrome."

She gaped at him. "Alena has what?"

Logan lowered his voice. "She was born without a uterus."

The bun dropped from Marigold's hand and landed in her lap. "What... what caused it?"

He shrugged. "Her doctor said it was a random genetic accident."

She wondered when Alena had told Logan about her condition. "Logi, I'm so sorry."

He stared at his hands. "There are uterus transplants being done in the US. Even though it's an experimental procedure, Alena had wanted to give it a try. When we called the hospital, they told us we'll need about half-a-million Canadian dollars."

She knew Logan and his wife didn't have that kind of money. "What's your next step?"

His eyes were sad when he looked up. "We're still exploring our options."

The desperation in his voice made her heart ache. "Is there anything I can do to help?"

"We can use a lot of prayers," he said.

She would do anything but that. "Logi, you know I don't do prayers. There has to be something else?"

Logan ran mustard-covered fingers through his thick auburn hair. "Alena's gone quiet on me. Mari, what am I going to do?"

She placed a comforting hand on his arm. What could she say?

CHAPTER THREE

After work, Marigold headed home. She turned on her blinker as she waited to make a left turn onto her street. The conversation with Logan weighed on her mind. Why couldn't life just be straightforward?

After she'd parked her car in front of the condo building, Marigold took the elevator up to the tenth floor. She gave a loud sigh of relief as she kicked off her shoes and dumped her purse on the couch.

By the time she turned the knob on her bedroom door, her clothes laid a trail on the carpet. Every time Logan came over and saw the messy condition of her apartment, he would tell her she'd turned into a citified slob. She loved the freedom of living on her own.

She flopped on her bed and stared up at the ceiling. On most days, the solitude calmed her. That evening, the quietness only amplified her racing thoughts. She stood, walked over to her closet, and dug out her gym clothes. She would have to tire herself out.

The elevator took her back to the building's first level. One of the perks of living at that address was their onsite gym. As usual, the room was half-empty. By Wednesday, most people were just hanging in until the weekend.

After she'd split her hour workout between weights and a spinning bike, she decided she'd had enough. On her way out of the gym, she ran into her friend, Archibong.

His round face lit up with a big smile. "My fine, Nigerian sister."

Marigold smiled. He gave her the dual citizenship status. "My stalker from the seventh floor."

Archibong's chiseled body pressed against hers when they exchanged a hug. His dedication to daily workouts had earned him a group of female admirers at the gym.

"I would have been here sooner if I'd had known you were working out tonight," he said.

She gave him an apologetic smile. "Last minute decision."

Archibong arched an eyebrow. "Are we still on for our movie date?"

She shuffled from one foot to the other. Archibong had wanted them to catch a movie at one of the new drive-in theaters. She loved the old school charm.

Marigold knew that if she were to indicate any romantic interest, Archibong would have her locked into an exclusive relationship before the end of that conversation. She preferred not to date someone living in her building. With her record, the relationship wouldn't last, and the proximity would make for an awkward breakup. "I'll let you know," she said.

Archibong looked a bit disappointed. "Okay."

She covered a yawn. "It's been a long day. I'll see you later."

"Goodnight."

Marigold leaned against the wall of the elevator as it sped up. The first time she met Archibong, he'd told her she looked like a younger version of his mother. Until Archibong produced his mother's picture, it'd sounded like an awful pickup line.

When she'd mentioned the startling similarity to Logan, he'd thought it would be fun for them to do a Genealogical DNA test.

Marigold's result identified her as 75.3% African. The 3.5% European ancestry explained the patch of straight, silky hair right in the middle of her kinky curls. The surprise was that the test also identified West Africa as one of her ethnicity regions.

Archibong said it was confirmation that one of her ancestors came from his tribe. When she'd asked if that made her a princess, he answered her with an emphatic, "No!"

While Logan's ancestry composition was predominately European, he also had 1.5% South Asian. As far as she was concerned, the pure race thing was as her grandmother would say, "Hogwash."

Marigold stepped out of the elevator when it reached her floor. The blinking message light on her answering machine caught her eye as soon as she walked into her apartment. Curious, she pressed the speaker button. The message was from her grandmother. As usual, Big Momma went straight to the point.

"Child, it's me. I hope you spoke to Ixora today. It's Jada's birthday. Call me when you get this message."

Marigold ran a hand over her face. She'd forgotten about her niece's birthday. It would be one more thing for her younger sister to complain about.

She sat on the couch with her cell phone, logged into her bank account, and sent Ixora an Interac e-Transfer. The attached message said the money was for Jada's birthday gift. She closed the browser and opened her Facetime app. Jada should still be awake.

The screen was dark when Ixora took her call. "Where are you?" Marigold asked.

"Hiding from Jada and her friends at Laser World. These kids don't play nice."

Marigold laughed. "Please tell Jada I said, Happy Birthday. I also sent her some money. I'm sure there's something she wants."

Ixora's whisper was fierce. "She wants to see you."

Marigold crossed her legs. Ixora and her family lived in Owen Sound. With the traffic, it was about a three-hour drive from Toronto. She also wanted to see her niece but that meant spending time with her sister. Ixora's constant criticism made the idea unattractive.

"Message received. In the meantime, I'm sure there's something you can *buy* for her."

Ixora sighed. "I guess."

"I have to call Big Momma. I'll talk to you later."

"Bye."

Marigold took a shower and changed into her pajamas before she called her grandmother. Depending on the day, their conversation could last up to an hour.

She opened up her Facetime app and dialed her grandmother's number. Big Momma thought Facetime was the best thing since auto GPS units.

"You got my message," Big Momma said after they'd exchanged hellos.

Big Momma's ladybug themed sleeping cap made her smile. "You look cute."

"Stop trying to butter me up. I'm sure you didn't call your sister before you got my message."

She hesitated. "Yes, I didn't."

Big Momma frowned. "Marigold."

An ex-librarian slash small scale, blueberry farmer, her grandmother did everything by the book. "In my defense, it's been a busy week," she said.

"You should have saved Jada's birthday on your phone and told that busybody, Siri, to send you a reminder. I've told you one is never too busy for family."

Marigold sighed. "Yes, Big Momma."

Her grandmother's expression softened. "Child, I've missed you. When are you coming to see me?"

Visits to Mapleville always brought memories she would rather forget. "It's been a while since you came to Toronto. Let me send you a train ticket."

Big Momma shook her head. "Come home."

"I'll see what I can do."

"What you can do is to get your stubborn behind into your car and drive west on Highway 401."

She smiled. "Yes, Big Momma."

Her grandmother blew her a kiss. "I love you."

Marigold made a show of catching the kiss and placing it against her cheek. "I love you, too."

After the call, she warmed up some leftover panzerotti, poured herself a big glass of red wine, and sat on the couch to watch the recorded episode of "Empire." There was only so much one person could deal with in a day.

CHAPTER FOUR

Marigold sat on the couch with her legs tucked under her as she dialed Archibong's number. She had to let him know that weekend wouldn't work for their movie date.

"Why not?" Archibong asked in a gruff voice.

"Logan's taking me to out to dinner. March 21st is our return to Canada anniversary."

"I can come along to even out the numbers," Archibong said.

"Alena isn't coming."

"Really?"

"Yes. It's not their anniversary."

Archibong snorted. "She must be a very understanding wife."

Marigold frowned. "What do you mean by that?"

"Well, if you were my girl, I wouldn't be comfortable with the amount of time you spend with Logan."

"Then it's a good thing I'm not," she said.

"Marigold."

"A man and a woman can just be best friends."

"That is true," Archibong said in a conciliatory tone.

Marigold took a deep breath. "You just like to get me all riled up, don't you?"

"It shouldn't be so easy to get under that beautiful skin," he said.

"And there you go again. Goodnight."

Archibong laughed. "Sweet dreams."

Marigold dropped the cell phone on her lap. Reason number two why Archibong needed to stay in the friend zone. She didn't like the way he could get past her defenses.

Saturday morning, Marigold woke up, brushed her teeth, and went to the gym. After a hot shower, she did some grocery shopping and picked up her red cocktail dress from the dry cleaners. She still didn't understand why a blind dining restaurant had a black tie dress code.

Marigold was ready by the time Logan called to say he was waiting in the lobby. She grabbed her purse, faux fur wrap, and went downstairs.

Logan gave a low whistle when she stepped out of the elevator. "Hello, gorgeous."

He was dressed in a navy tuxedo. "You don't look half bad yourself."

When they arrived at Sentir, a hostess welcomed them at the restaurant's waiting area. A pair of night vision goggles was strapped to her forehead. "Thanks for honoring the dress code. At Sentir, we want to engage your other senses, so it's not about how you look in a dress or suit, it's about how you feel in it."

Logan grinned as he adjusted his tie. "I feel ready for an adventure," he said.

The waitress smiled. "Then you should order a meal from our "Surprise Me" menu."

"Done," Logan said.

The waitress turned in her direction.

Marigold smiled. "I'm going with the steak."

"Great choice. Please follow me. My colleagues will seat you at your table."

They were paired with waiters who led them by hand into the pitch dark dining room. Disoriented, Marigold was grateful when she reached out and felt a wall.

As they made their way through the room, she noted that the conversation was louder than she was used to at a restaurant. Perhaps people were compensating for the temporary sight loss. She sat and the stiff edges of the linen tablecloth draped across her lap.

"You're okay?" Logan asked after she sighed.

"This feels unsettling," she said.

"Just relax. Once in a while, it's good to live on the edge."

She'd been living on the edge for as long as she could remember. If she moved just one more inch, she was sure to fall over. She explored the table with her hands. "They gave us plastic cups."

"They probably don't want guests hurting themselves with glass shards," Logan said.

"True."

When the waiter brought a basket of warm bread rolls, Marigold managed to open the small butter container without getting it all over her hand. "This experience gives me a better understanding of the challenges blind people face."

"The website said all the waiters are blind or visually impaired," Logan said.

"That's a great idea."

"So, how's your food?" he asked after the waiter had served their meals.

Unable to see her plate, she'd concentrated on the flavors and textures. "Very good. How's the surprise meal?"

"There are potatoes on my plate, but I'm not sure if this is chicken breast or veal. Whatever it is, I'm open to seconds."

Marigold's ears perked up when Rod Stewart's, "Beyond the Sea" began playing over the restaurant's sound system. "Remember that song?"

She heard the smile in Logan's voice. "Of course."

One year, she and Logan had worked in the entertainment department of an adults' only cruise ship. They had a live band on board. She remembered the old men who had to be told to keep their hands on her waist during ballroom dancing. "Do you miss our old life?"

Logan took his time to respond. "I'm where I'm supposed to be," he said.

Marigold was sure she wasn't. Even though she'd become accustomed to the ship's movement, each day she wasn't sure where she'd been the day before. Now it felt as if she was stuck on a carousel, same people, same pace, and the same boring views. "I've been thinking of going back to sea."

"Why?"

"There's nothing to keep me here. You're all settled. And, I'm sure your wife would love to have you all to herself."

"Alena doesn't see you as a threat."

Marigold gave a wry smile. "If you say so."

"I'm serious. Remember, you'd asked if there was anything you could do about the baby issue?"

"Yes?"

She heard Logan exhale. "Well, Alena and I were wondering if you would act as our surrogate mother."

Marigold dropped her cutlery against the plate. They wanted her to carry their baby?

"Are you still there?"

"I didn't see that coming."

"Mari, I know it's a huge commitment. It's almost a year of your life."

Logan was worth more than that to her. She had heard of people using donor eggs. "The baby would be yours and mine?"

"No. Our baby, your womb."

Speechless, Marigold stared into the darkness. When she had asked Logan if there was anything else she could do to help, surrogacy had not crossed her mind.

"I shouldn't have asked in the middle of dinner. I'm sorry."

"Logi, I don't know what to say."

"I wasn't expecting you to give me an on the spot answer. At the very least, sleep on it."

The tight feeling in her chest eased. "Okay."

"Don't feel bad if you have to say no. You have to think about yourself."

Marigold's fingers clenched around her plastic cup. During a heated argument with Ixora, her sister had declared that Marigold had a hard time with relationships because she was selfish.

There wasn't anything bad about being focused on her needs and priorities. Why should she love someone on their own terms? "According to Ixora, that's all I do," she said.

"I want us to enjoy the rest of our dinner. So, no more talk about babies and little sisters. Deal?"

Marigold took a deep breath. "Deal."

CHAPTER FIVE

It was late by the time Marigold returned to her apartment. She changed out of her cocktail dress and sat in the front of the television. As she flipped through the channels, she thought about Logan's request. After all he had done for her, how could she say no?

Alena's face came to her mind. Marigold had always imagined that she, Logan, and their spouses would be the fantastic four, awesome aunts and uncles to each other's children. In their unstated battle for Logan's attention, she and Alena had barely spoken. How could she carry a baby for a woman she didn't even like?

The green light on the coffee maker had just turned on when Marigold's cell phone rang. She picked it up from the counter, looked at the screen. It was Logan. She growled into the phone. "What do you want? You know I'm not a morning person."

"Hello, Marigold. It's Alena."

The sound of Alena's voice made her lean against the counter. "Is Logan okay?"

"Yes. He's right beside me. Is it possible for you to meet me for lunch?"

Alena must have changed Logan's mind about the surrogacy. Marigold poured herself a cup of scalding, black coffee and took a sip before she responded. "Sure."

"Is there a particular place you'll like to go?"

"No. Just tell me where to meet you."

"You know the strip mall at Lawrence Avenue West and Black Creek Drive?"

It wasn't too far from her place. "Yes."

"There's a nice Italian bistro there."

She needed time to mentally prepare herself. "If you don't mind a late lunch, I'll meet you there at one."

"That's fine. Thank you."

Marigold arrived half an hour early for the lunch date. She was seated at a back table by the time Alena arrived.

"Hey," Alena said with a half-smile as she pulled out her chair.

"Hey. I chose this table because I thought we might need some privacy," she said.

"Good call."

After they'd ordered some appetizers, she gave Alena an expectant look. "So, what's up?"

Alena lifted her chin. "Logan told me he had asked you to be our surrogate mother."

"Yes, he did."

"Well, I know you don't like me," Alena said.

Marigold squirmed in her seat. She had not expected the candid statement. "We've had our differences," she said.

Alena raised an eyebrow. "What exactly have I done to you?"

She couldn't admit to her jealousy. "To be honest, nothing major."

"Logan wants you to be our surrogate. I'm fine with that. If you agree to this, we'll have to spend a lot of time together. I need to know that it wouldn't be like doing a stint in hell."

"From what I remember from Sunday school, we're talking fire and brimstone. The experience wouldn't even be close," she said.

Alena cleared her throat. "Even if your answer is no, I hope this can be a new beginning for us."

She was willing to try. "We're both adults. We can make this work."

Alena looked relieved. "I'm sure Logan didn't talk to you about the money details."

"He didn't. But I don't need to be paid for helping you guys out."

"We can't even pay if you'd wanted us to. It's illegal. We can cover the costs of your maternity clothes, vitamins, pretty much anything else you need to buy."

"I can buy my own stuff. From what I read on the Internet you'll have a lot to pay for."

"We do. But if you agree to this, I'll...I mean we'll feel better if we can cover some of those costs."

Marigold shrugged. "Just trying to help."

Alena stared at her hands. "This whole process is very hard for me. Thanks for meeting with me."

Marigold felt a twinge of pity. "My pleasure."

She heard Alena take a deep breath. "Let us know when you have an answer."

Marigold nodded. "Will do."

After twelve days of thinking and avoiding Logan's eyes at work, Marigold made up her mind. She was sure of two things. She loved Logan. She also owed him. There were other people he could use as a surrogate, but he chose her. Logan's request was also an opportunity for her to prove to her sister that she did have a selfless side.

She called Logan at home. "Done enough thinking. Let's do this."

"Is this impulsive Marigold talking?" Logan asked.

The last things she needed were more doubts. "You don't want me to do this?"

"I do. I just don't want you to have any regrets," he said.

"If I get covered in stretch marks, I'm going to blame you, but my answer is still yes."

Logan gave a loud cheer. "Baby, she said yes! Mari said yes."

Alena came on the phone. She sounded as if she was crying. "Thank you so much."

"You're welcome. When do you want to get this started?"

"We'll work around your schedule."

Marigold did the math. If things went well, they would be looking at a winter baby. By the time spring came around, she would be ready to leave town. "How soon can we see your doctor?"

"I'll call the clinic and let you know," Alena said.

After ending the call, Marigold closed her eyes as she rested her head against the pillow. A winter baby meant not taking trips to Mapleville for Thanksgiving or Christmas. And Big Momma wanted to see her.

She blew out some air. This path to sainthood wasn't going to be as easy as it looked.

CHAPTER SIX

Later in the week, the three of them met with the reproductive endocrinologist at Alena's fertility clinic. With Logan between her and Alena, their straight-backed chairs stood opposite the doctor's cluttered desk.

Marigold's head ached. The doctor had used visuals to explain the in vitro-fertilization process. What she understood was that after Logan and Alena had done the egg collection and fertilization procedures, they would move into the embryo transfer. While they were doing their thing, she had to go through a physical and psychological evaluation. The doctor was clear that another surrogate would be needed if the evaluations identified that pregnancy would pose a risk to Marigold's health.

The doctor gave them a serious look. "We're hoping and preparing for the best. But complications happen. I think it's important that you seek legal advice with regards to a preconception agreement. The contract protects everyone."

Alena glanced at her husband. "We'll speak to a lawyer," she said.

The doctor gave Marigold a kind smile. "This is going to be an emotionally taxing process so I'm recommending regular sessions with one of our staff counselors. Feedback from other surrogates highlights the service as an invaluable support."

Right after the plane crash, Big Momma took her and Ixora to see a counselor. While Ixora couldn't stop talking, she didn't want to be there. For months, all she did was sit on the couch and spend the hour playing Pac-Man on a Nintendo Game Boy. The counselor said her parents were now her guardian angels. Like that mattered when all she wanted was the opportunity to say sorry to her mother for the mean things she'd said before they left.

Marigold forced a smile. She knew how to give the right responses. "I'll book a session."

The night before the embryo transfer, Logan showed up at Marigold's place with two huge gift baskets. "I know you said you didn't need anything. But we wanted to spoil you a little."

"What am I meant to do with all this stuff?"

"Sit down and take a look. There are some practical things in there."

One basket was a spa and relaxation delight: soaps, lotions, a gel neck pillow, lavender bags, bath oil, face washer, loofahs, massage tools, a giant Sudoku book, the latest editions of Chatelaine and Cosmopolitan, and three pregnancy test kits.

The second basket had snacks: cookies, chocolate bars, dried fruit, gourmet cheese, peanut brittle, and caramel nut crunch. She looked up at Logan. "No wine?"

"Very funny."

She grinned. "Thank you for the goodies. That woman of yours has taste."

"Of course, she does. She saw me and was like, that dude is mine!"

Marigold rested her back against the couch. "It must feel good to live in a deluded world."

He held out his hand. "Join us. Delusion craves company."

"No, thank you."

Logan smiled. "Are you ready for tomorrow?"

She wasn't. "Working on it. I do have a battle cry."

"What is it?"

Marigold stood, held up her fist, and struck a defiant pose as she recited "Invictus" by William Ernest Henley.

Out of the night that covers me,
Black as the pit from pole to pole,
I thank whatever gods may be
For my unconquerable soul.
In the fell clutch of circumstance
I have not winced nor cried aloud.
Under the bludgeonings of chance
My head is bloody but unbowed.
Beyond this place of wrath and tears
Looms but the Horror of the shade,
And yet the menace of the years
Finds and shall find me unafraid.
It matters not how strait the gate,
How charged with punishments the scroll,
I am the master of my fate,
I am the captain of my soul.

Logan clapped when she curtsied. "You still remember the words. But are we really the masters of our fate? I think we humans control less than we think. Life is easier when we accept that."

She shook her head. "For the record, I'm the mistress. And I think your statement reeks of cowardice."

"Is that so?" Logan said as he reached for the afghan thrown across the couch. He stood and wrapped it around his body like a toga.

Marigold shook her head. "What are you doing?

Logan held his arm straight in front of him with his palm turned down. "Cowards may die many times before their deaths, and the valiant may never taste of death but once. Still, give me the shield of cowardice that I may balance on it my fresh coconut drink."

Marigold snickered. In high school, they'd acted in, *Julius Caesar*. Logan thought drama class was fun. She'd wanted to escape into an imaginary world. "Are you saying Caesar visited the Caribbean?"

He ignored her question. "For if death doth tarry, the tales of victorious exploits floweth not from the silent grave of the valiant but from the mouths of those who hid and lived to tell the tale."

Marigold flapped her arms and made chicken noises.

Logan stuck out his tongue as he unwrapped himself and sat back on the couch. "Remember our plans for the Logi and Mari Show? It's not too late."

"Not while you're trying to have a baby."

"A baby can travel with us. Alena would be great at makeup and costume."

Marigold raised an eyebrow. "Are you serious?"

He grinned. "No. We're almost thirty. Time to be a proper adult."

"Adults don't chase their dreams?"

"They do. Are you saying you really want to start this show?"

Marigold shook her head. "I just enjoy talking about it."

"That's one of the things I love about you. You never stop exploring. I've become a settler. Give me a comfy chair, a remote, food, and I'm not moving."

"Well, Mr. van Basten, that's just too bad."

Logan stood. "I should be heading home."

"I was about to kick you out. I need to shave my legs."

Logan laughed. "I don't think that's what the doctor will be looking at."

"I didn't see a ring on his finger. So, you never know."

At the door, Logan kissed her on the forehead. "You're the best person anyone can have in their corner."

Marigold swallowed the lump in her throat. He wasn't going to make her cry. "Goodnight. Drive safe."

CHAPTER SEVEN

Dressed in matching T-shirts, Logan and Alena rose from their seats when Marigold walked into the clinic's waiting room. "Good morning, people."

"You're here!" Alena said as if she'd thought Marigold was on her way to the New York state border.

Marigold inclined her head towards the wall clock. "Our appointment is still an hour away."

Alena looked embarrassed. "We've been here for a while. I'm just too excited."

Logan put an arm around his wife's shoulders. "I know I look all calm outside but inside, I'm squealing, too."

She narrowed her eyes. "Well, I need to maintain my Zen mood so I'm just going to sit over there and distract myself with the giant Sudoku book you guys gave me."

Logan made a zipping gesture across his mouth. "You won't hear a word from us."

By the time the nurse came for them, Marigold was wondering if it was too late to head for the border. Changed into a hospital gown, her legs were fastened in the medical stirrups at the end of the bed before the embryo was wheeled into the transfer room with an incubator. Even though they had three viable embryos, the plan was to implant them one at a time.

As agreed, Logan and Alena were in the room. She'd asked that they stay far away from the foot of the bed. There would be no peeking.

The doctor looked up at her. "Relax. This is going to be quick."

"So what's your plan for the weekend?" the nurse beside Marigold asked.

"The weekend?" Marigold asked as if the word was foreign to her.

"It is Friday."

She was supposed to stay on bedrest for three days. "I think I'm going dancing."

"Oh, no, you're not," Alena said in a raised voice.

"You don't want to cross her, Mari," Logan said.

Marigold sighed. "Spoilsport. Fine. I'll stay home."

The doctor was right about timing. The procedure took ten minutes, and Marigold had only experienced some mild discomfort. After two hours of rest at the clinic, she was free to leave.

Alena and Logan drove her home. She went straight to bed.

"Do you need anything else?" Logan asked after he'd covered her with the duvet.

Marigold shook her head. "I'm fine."

"Would you like to eat?" Alena asked. "Logan will bring the meal."

It felt uncomfortable to have both of them in her bedroom. "Maybe some spaghetti and spicy Italian sausage?"

Alena cleared her throat. "I read that spicy foods are not good for pregnant women."

Marigold counted to ten in her head. "Don't bother. I have some cooked food."

"I can make you a cup of tea?" Alena offered.

Marigold was ready to be alone. "No, thank you. I'll just stay in bed and think good thoughts."

"We'll let ourselves out," Logan said.

Marigold waited until they'd closed the bedroom door behind them before she began to cry. If someone had been in the room, she wouldn't have been able to explain why.

When she was spent, she touched her wet cheek. It had been a while since she'd done the ugly crying thing. Maybe she was pregnant already.

The weeks after the transfer crawled. As she ticked each day off her wall calendar, Marigold tried not to think about going back for another embryo transfer.

On day fifteen, Logan and Alena were back at her place for the pregnancy test reveal. Wrapped in a paper towel, she'd placed the wand on the pile of grocery bags spread on her little stool. They had to wait for three minutes.

"I think it's time," Logan said as he snapped on the disposable gloves Marigold gave him.

Marigold stood. As much as she wanted to stay in the room, it was their moment, not hers. "I'll be in the kitchen."

Her fingers were crossed when she heard Logan cry out. "It worked! Alena, look! It worked."

She peeked out from the kitchen and watched as Logan and Alena clung to each other in the middle of her living room. All she heard from Alena were deep moans.

Marigold turned away and leaned against her kitchen wall. She was pregnant. Her hand rested on her flat stomach. This was the best outcome. Why was she suddenly overcome with dread?

CHAPTER EIGHT

Marigold was still trying to wrap her mind around the changes ahead when Alena and Logan came back with more gifts.

Alena gave her the little potted tree. "A bonsai represents peace, balance, and harmony. I thought you would like it," she said.

Marigold stared at the plant thinking, *Great, another living thing to care for*. "Thank you."

Logan gave her their second present. The sterling silver, kangaroo charm from Pandora's had a small joey kangaroo in its pouch. Marigold smiled. "This is precious."

"We wanted to get something for our special kangaroo," Logan said. "And I say that with love."

Marigold chuckled. At Christmas, Logan gave her a Pandora bracelet and a cruise ship charm. "Sure," she said.

"Female kangaroos are very protective of their babies, so we know you'll take care of ours," Alena said.

"It still feels very surreal," Marigold said.

Logan nodded. "When I woke up this morning, I had to check that wand again."

"We can't thank you enough," Alena said before she left to use the bathroom. Logan stayed in the room.

Marigold unclasped her Pandora bracelet. "This is really nice. I'll have to check out their other charms."

"Let me put that on for you," Logan said after she'd added the kangaroo charm.

"We should do this again after this baby turns three," she said.

Logan snorted. "I don't think my weak nerves or shallow pockets can handle it. Mari, I can't believe I'm going to be a dad."

She smiled at him. There was a part of Logan's hair which stuck out no matter how many times he combed it. She stretched her hand and patted it down. "You're going to make a great one."

"Am I interrupting something?"

Marigold looked up at the sound of Alena's voice. At the sight of Alena's scowl, she snatched her hand away from Logan's head. "Not at all."

Logan gave his wife a puzzled look. "What?"

Alena sat next to Logan and gave Marigold a close-lipped smile as she did a proprietary caress of his thigh. "Never mind, honey."

Marigold returned Alena's smile. *Message received.*

Marigold knew she had to tell Archibong about the pregnancy before it began to show. A dinner date at her place felt like a good opportunity.

Archibong didn't hide his excitement when he walked in with dessert. "I come to you with a cleansed palette," he said with a dramatic bow after he'd sat at the dining table.

"We're just having chili and buckwheat rolls," she said.

Archibong grinned. "Your hot presence adds an extra layer of habanero cheese on everything."

Marigold passed the butter dish. "You really need to work on your pick up lines."

He gave her a wink. "If I do, you'll be my girl?"

She could tell that he was serious. "Right now, if I were to say yes to your question, you would be getting a girl and a baby."

He blinked. "A baby?"

"I'm pregnant."

Archibong looked as if he'd been sucker punched. "Who is this guy? How come I've never met him?"

She shrugged. "It's complicated."

"How so?"

"He's not available for a relationship. It was just a ten-minute thing."

Archibong stood. "I think I'll take a raincheck on the dinner."

Why did she feel so bad? "I'm sorry."

Archibong sighed. "I'm sorry, too."

After two months of prolonged morning sickness, Marigold was finally able to catch a whiff of the foods she had loved without feeling sick to her stomach.

"Logi, Jr., what do you think we should eat today?" Marigold said aloud as she opened the freezer door. Conversations with the baby no longer felt weird after she'd given it a name. She began talking to Logi, Jr. after Mommy Alena told her talking to a baby in the womb was a good thing. They already had classical music time. She was going to do everything she could to make sure the baby had the best start.

Marigold scanned the labeled Tupperware containers Alena brought over. They'd agreed that Alena would make her meals since she loved to cook, and she wanted to feel like she was contributing something to her baby's growth. She wrinkled her nose as she read the labels. Nothing looked interesting. She slammed the freezer door shut.

Despite the potential for some serious heartburn, what she really wanted was a bowl of Archibong's pepper soup. Their mother had raised her and Ixora on spicy gumbo and chili, but she wasn't prepared for the heat in the Nigerian dish. It had felt as if her body was on fire. She had to drink a whole container of milk to cool her tongue.

She changed out of her house robe into a comfortable tracksuit. It was time to shop for some pregnancy clothes.

Marigold gave herself a quick glance in the mirror. Even though Archibong had stayed away from her, she didn't think he would say no to a pregnant woman's desperate plea.

Archibong's eyes popped when he opened his door. "Wowzer! You've been eating a lot of pecans."

She gave him a half-smile. The funny thing was that she could no longer stand the nuts. "I'm now an almond girl. Can I come in?"

Archibong hesitated before he held the door open. Relieved, she walked in. "Are you okay?" he asked after he'd closed the door behind them.

Marigold shook her head. "I need some pepper soup."

Archibong chuckled. "You want some pepper soup?"

"My brother, abeg, this is a need. The baby's bringing out my West African side," she said.

He smiled. "You're now using Nigerian slangs?"

"A side effect of hanging out with you. Man, do you have some pepper soup in your fridge?"

"Hmm. My provision of pepper soup has one condition. I get to give the baby a proper Efik naming ceremony."

He would have to deal with Logan and Alena. "Fine with me as long as you can deliver pepper soup bowls on a regular basis."

Archibong shook his head. "Sit your hungry self at the dining table. I'll be right back."

CHAPTER NINE

"What's going on between you two?" Ziva asked with an arched eyebrow.

Seated at her desk, Marigold frowned. "What do you mean?"

Ziva turned to Logan. "Dude, is that your baby in Marigold's stomach?"

She gave Logan a warning look. *Alena will kill you if you share her business.*

"It's not what you think," Logan said as he stepped away from Marigold's desk.

Wide-eyed, Ziva placed a hand over her opened mouth. "Ooh, you guys are knocking boots."

Ziva grew up on an Alberta cow ranch. "Girl, your imagination needs to be reined in," Marigold said.

Ziva squinted her eyes at Logan. "Does your wife know?"

"This isn't any of your business," Logan said in a terse tone.

"I've always suspected that gold ring on your finger was just a placeholder," Ziva said to Logan before she turned to her. "And your Big Momma must be so proud."

She glared at Ziva. "Why did you have to bring my grandmother into this?"

Logan was on his feet by the time she pulled herself up from her chair. "Mari, no."

She gave him the stink eye. What did he think she was going to do? "I'm not planning to have this baby in a jail cell."

In the bathroom, Marigold splashed some water on her face and took a deep breath. On weekday mornings when Logan said hello to her stomach, it was easy to pretend that the baby in her stomach belonged to them. Easy but foolish. She dried her face. They did need to keep all baby talk out of the office.

She came out of the single-stall bathroom and met Ziva out in the hallway.

Ziva gave her an apologetic look. "What I said was way out of line. I'm sorry."

"It was. And for the record, Logan and I not having an affair. He loves his wife."

Ziva sighed. "I know this will change things between us."

She wasn't in a forgiving mood. "We should get back to work," Marigold said.

Ziva opened and closed her mouth before she turned and walked away.

Marigold had just managed to calm down when her cell phone rang. It was Ixora. "Hey, Sis. I'm in Toronto."

"What brings you to the city?"

"Eli's here for a conference at the Harbourfront Centre. I thought it was the perfect opportunity to see you. Are you free for lunch?"

If she said no, Ixora might stop by at the office. They'd had enough drama for the day. "Sure. I'll meet you at Tim Hortons just down the street from the Centre."

Marigold heard the smile in Ixora's voice "See you soon," she said.

At the coffee shop, Ixora took one look at Marigold's stomach and sat back down.

Marigold gave an internal chuckle. It was good to know something could curb Ixora's tongue. She sat across from her sister. "You look good."

"And you look pregnant."

"Wow. No hello, you just went straight to insult time."

The confused look on Ixora's face deepened. "You're not pregnant?"

"I am."

Ixora's eyes flashed. "Then what are you talking about?"

This wasn't how to show Ixora that she'd changed. "This isn't my child. I'm a surrogate."

Ixora blinked. "A surrogate?"

"Yes."

"Where did you find this person?"

"A couple. Logan and Alena."

Ixora's eyes grew big. "No way. You've had nothing good to say about Alena."

Marigold felt a twinge of shame. If Logan knew about all the unflattering names she had called his wife, he wouldn't be happy with her. Now that she had been spending more time with Alena, she was getting to like her. "Those are not some of my proudest moments."

"How far along are you?"

"Four months," she said.

Ixora gave a long sigh. "Does Big Momma know you're pregnant?"

During their last Facetime call, Big Momma had commented about her larger nose. "No. And you can't tell her. Logan told his parents they were using a surrogate, but he didn't say it was me. You know how his mom feels about me."

Ixora still looked stunned. "You won't have a problem with handing over the baby?"

Marigold rested a hand on her stomach. Every day she had to remind herself that the baby wasn't hers. The only consolation was that she would be able to watch the child grow. "No."

"I don't know what to say."

How about way to go, Big Sis. You do care about other people.

"For a long time, I've wanted to know my purpose. Maybe this is it. I can help other women become mothers."

Ixora continued to stare at her.

Marigold gave a nervous laugh. "I'm not saying I'm going to keep getting pregnant. Who does that? The details are still fuzzy.

But it would be an online thing where surrogates and families find each other. What do you think?"

Ixora stood. "Your lunch hour will be over soon. What would you like?"

She had lost her appetite but Logi, Jr. had to eat. The baby was usually active after mealtimes. "A grilled Tuscan chicken panini and a bottle of water. Please."

"I'll be right back."

Marigold pursed her lips as she watched her sister walk away. Dressed in a blue-gray pantsuit, Ixora looked like the successful business woman that she was. Nothing she did was going to be good enough to impress her.

"How did the lunch with your sister go?" Logan asked when she returned to the office.

"You know how she is. Mistress of Criticism."

Logan shook his head. "Ixora's horns grow more pointed every time you talk about her."

Marigold pursed her lips. "I say it as it is."

"Sometimes, it's best not to say anything," Logan said with a soft smile before he walked away.

The smile didn't take the sting out of Logan's words. She stared at his back. Easy for him to say when things always worked out for him.

CHAPTER TEN

Two weeks after Ixora's visit, they were back in the doctor's office to hear the result of the amniocentesis test the doctor ordered. He'd wanted to make sure there were no chromosomal disorders.

Marigold could tell there was something off when the three of them walked into the room. While the doctor gave them a smile, his eyes retained their somber look.

"Please, is everything okay?" Alena asked. She was quiet during their drive to the clinic.

"I'm so sorry," the doctor said. "There was an abnormality in the result."

Marigold held on to the arms of her chair. "What does that mean?" she asked.

"It means that the fetus has Down Syndrome." The doctor rattled off the challenges: learning delays, congenital heart defects, low muscle, amongst other things.

Marigold rested a hand on her stomach as the room spun. *No.*

The doctor turned to Logan and Alena. "Perhaps we should have a private discussion about available options?"

Alena began to sob. "This is so unfair."

Marigold frowned. "What options?"

The doctor glanced at Logan. He continued to stare into space. "I really should be having the conversation with the parents."

Marigold gave him a steely look. She could feel Logi, Jr. moving inside her. "Since any decision would affect me, I'm not leaving the room."

The doctor turned to Alena. "Under the current laws, the gestational carrier does have rights over the unborn child until the time of birth. But the preconception contract you signed would have covered this kind of situation."

Marigold remembered the conversation about a preconception contract. "I didn't sign anything," she said.

Alena shook her husband's arm. "Logan!"

"What?" He looked dazed.

"You told me Marigold signed the contract."

His face flushed. "I couldn't make her do it. She's my best friend."

Alena rose to her feet. "And I'm your wife!"

Logan ran his fingers through his hair. "I didn't know things would turn out this way."

"Why do you keep choosing her over me?" Alena asked before she ran out of the room.

Logan gave her a sad look before he ran after his wife.

Marigold didn't move until the doctor tapped her on the arm. "I'm sorry, but I have another appointment. If you drove here, I think you should tell the secretary to call you a cab. You shouldn't drive in this state."

She held on to the chair and pulled herself up. "What options do we have?"

"A termination of the pregnancy."

The words felt like a vicious kick in the shin. The child she saw during the 3D ultrasound had a beating heart. "You want me to terminate someone's life?"

The doctor pursed his lips. "We're talking about a fetus."

His flippant tone took Marigold's breath. "Wow. You must have missed your patient sensitivity training."

The doctor opened his mouth. She didn't give him the opportunity to express the annoyance visible on his face. "We're talking about a child. A child that you helped bring into this world."

He was silent as Marigold walked out of the office.

Marigold blinked her tear-filled eyes as she drove home. Her grandmother's somber face came to her mind. She remembered the memorial held months after her parent's plane went missing, Big Momma's words about how they'd lost three people not two. Her mother had shared the news of her surprise pregnancy just before they left for their trip.

Logan sent her a text message when she arrived at home: *Are you okay?*

Curled in bed, Marigold stared at the screen. The look of betrayal on Alena's face was painful to see. But Logan had tried to protect her. She typed a response: *We need to talk.*

Logan responded: *I know. Tomorrow?*

It was best to have the conversation as soon as possible: *See you at seven.*

Marigold placed the cell phone on her dresser and closed her eyes. She remembered how Alena and Logan had celebrated the positive pregnancy test result. They wanted this child. *Everything will be fine.*

The next day, both Logan and Alena arrived at her doorstep with bloodshot eyes. Unable to sleep, she had called in sick and stayed home. They declined her offer of a drink and sat on the opposite couch. Marigold noted their held hands.

"The doctor called me," Alena said.

She wasn't surprised. "And?"

"He said he'd mentioned a termination."

The word made everything all sound clinical. "I'm sure he told you what I said."

Alena licked her lips as she glanced at her husband. "We still have two viable eggs. A termination would be in everyone's best interest."

Logi, Jr. would disagree. Marigold shook her head. "I can't."

Alena glared at her. "What do you mean by, you can't? You're talking to superficial, flaky Alena. Now, you think I have the strength to raise a child with special needs?"

Marigold held Alena's gaze. Before their marriage, she had typed the words in a text message to Logan. She didn't know that Alena saw it. "I'm sorry for the things I've said. But they have nothing to do with this child."

"You can't force us to raise a child we don't want," Alena said.

"And you can't force me to terminate the pregnancy." She turned to Logan. He knew about her mother. "You're in agreement with this?"

He hung his head. "I caused this mess."

Tears ran down Alena's face. "You think this is easy for me? Listen. When my friends started their periods, as icky as they said they were, I'd wanted to get them, too. The few times I told people about my disorder, they'd looked at me as if I was a freak. There were times I wanted to hurt myself. I didn't because I learned that if I didn't talk about it, no one would know that I was different. Marigold, we can't hide this child's difference. Everyone who sees those facial features will know. And they will judge. You heard what the doctor said. Why would I inflict such pain on someone I love?"

"Alena, I'm not trying to punish you. You don't have to raise the child. This morning, I spoke to a lawyer. Since I've decided to keep the baby, I think it's only fair for us to sign a contract which would absolve you and Logan of any responsibility towards the baby."

Alena gaped. "You're serious?"

"Yes. You'll be free to move on with your other viable options."

Logan stood from the couch. "How are you going to take care of the child on your own?"

As she stared at him, the pain in Marigold's heart intensified. *I did this for you.* "I'll figure things out."

Pale, Alena swayed as she stood from the couch. Her husband held her. "Our lawyer will be in touch," he said.

Marigold stared at Logan's somber face. *Did I ever really know you?*

CHAPTER ELEVEN

Marigold knew she should be looking for a new gynecologist, searching for appropriate services, making plans for an uncertain future, but her mind was a mess.

After two more sick days at home, she met with their boss, Ayesha, and handed in her resignation. She couldn't sit across from Logan and pretend everything was well.

Before she left the office she asked Logan if he would go for a walk with her. He agreed. They ended up at the park across from the food truck, at the picnic table where they'd sat when it all began.

"I'm sorry, Mari. Alena doesn't want the baby. I had lied to her about the contract. I have to make things right."

She'd known that Logan wouldn't go against his wife. He was a promise keeper. "I just handed in my resignation."

He gave a heavy sigh. "What are you going to do?"

While Ixora's share of the insurance compensation given to them by the airline had paid for her sister's education and wedding, hers had been left untouched in a bank account. "I don't know. I do have enough savings, so I'm going to be fine."

"I'm sorry."

A wave of grief wrapped around her as she blinked back her tears. A child needs a home with a stable, loving parent. Not a nine-month commitment. Not someone like her. "These apologies should go to your abandoned child," she said.

Logan winced. "I deserve that."

"I need my key back," she said.

Logan's hands shook as he pulled the key from his bunch. "You'll let me know if you need anything, right?"

He'd lost the privilege to be a part of her life. "No."

Logan sent the baby things they had bought to her place. Marigold stood by the door and watched the delivery guys stack the items in her spare bedroom.

At her request, they moved some of her old suitcases out. After they left, she rolled one of the suitcases to the living room. As far as she remembered, it held some of the things she'd left behind in Big Momma's house. The suitcase had books, rolled up wall posters, and some of the sea shells she'd collected when their family lived in Victoria.

Her breath caught when she saw an embossed purple journal. It usually sat next to her mother's study Bible. On that morning because of their fight, Mom forgot to pack it.

Marigold flipped through the pages. She hadn't known that it was a memory journal. In the daily gratitude section, Marigold couldn't count how many times her mother had written about something fun they had done together and how she was grateful for her.

Overwhelmed, she placed the journal on the couch and reached into the cardboard box. The sight of her old ribbon sticks made her exhale. The purple crushed ribbon still looked new.

Marigold stood. Her swollen fingers wrapped around the handles, she moved to the music which had started playing in her head. As the ribbons flew in the air, their tips fluttered around her like butterfly wings.

For a moment, she was back in the basement of the church in Victoria. It was practice time and twelve-year-old Marigold's tulle skirt twirled as she danced for the Jesus she'd accepted into her heart at the age of ten.

As her lips formed the words from, "I Need Thee Every Hour." Tears welled behind Marigold's closed eyelids. Was she still worthy?

The Lord your God is with you, the Mighty Warrior who saves. He will take great delight in you; in His love He will no longer rebuke you but will rejoice over you with singing.

Marigold's eyes flew open. The words were as clear as a bell. "You still take delight in me?"

I loved you before the creation of the world.

Marigold stepped out on the seventh floor and headed for Archibong's apartment. He looked a little distracted when he finally came to the door. "Sorry, I have a guest."

"Bongie, who is it?" Marigold heard a woman ask from inside Archibong's apartment.

Archibong glanced over his shoulder. "A friend. I'll be right back."

Before Archibong closed the door behind him, Marigold caught a glimpse of his guest. It was one of his admirers from the gym. She raised an eyebrow. "Bongie?"

He shrugged. "She was going to go with Bong. I'd noticed that your car has been parked in the same spot for the past week. You're okay?"

Marigold nodded. "See why I call you a stalker?"

Archibong held her gaze. "I didn't stop caring for you."

Marigold averted her eyes. "I'm leaving town for a while. And I was wondering if you could take care of my plant while I'm gone."

"You want me to babysit a plant?"

"It's going to need water and some pampering."

Archibong shook his head. "I've suffered in this Canada o."

He had told her Nigerians add 'o' to the end of their sentences. She held out the pot. "This pregnant woman's patience is wearing thin o."

Archibong laughed as he took the pot from her. "Why didn't you ask Logan?"

Marigold bit on her lower lip. "We no longer... em... he can't."

He glanced at her stomach. "I see."

She took a deep breath. "Thank you."

Archibong scratched his head. "Where are you going?"

All week the words *go home* had kept coming to her mind. Big Momma knew about loss. Maybe she could help her piece her life back together. Marigold pulled her sweater across her chest. "To my grandmother's place."

"When are you coming back?"

The length of her stay in Mapleville would depend on Big Momma's reception. "Not sure. But I should be back before the delivery date. The baby still needs that Efik name."

Archibong gave her a soft smile as he held the potted plant to his body. "I'm going to miss you."

She was going to miss him, too. "Take care, Bongie."

Archibong gave her a wink before he closed the door.

CHAPTER TWELVE

Marigold's pulse raced when she saw the large bronze "Welcome to Mapleville" sign by the side of the road. Her journey took longer than usual because of her many bathroom breaks. The child had to be sitting on her bladder.

A cloud of gravel dust rose from the tires as she swerved onto the road leading to her grandmother's house. Distracted by the thoughts of how to break the news to Big Momma, she'd almost missed the turn.

Parked at the end of the driveway, Marigold began her prodigal waddle to the ninety-year-old farmhouse.

The crunch of gravel under her shoes brought memories of the many times she had skipped up the road and the days she had run down it under a cloud of anger.

Right next to the house, Big Momma's new car looked like it'd just been washed. There were still beads of water on the shiny hood.

When their grandmother's station wagon died after decades of faithful service, she and Ixora gave her the car as an early seventieth birthday present. They had thought it would be funny to watch a petite, old woman with a gray afro bounce out of a neon yellow, Honda Fit with "Big Momma" personalized plates.

Since their grandmother wasn't a fan of vanity in any form, Ixora's children had handed her the keys. Big Momma couldn't say no to them.

She heard music and singing from open windows. Grandma must be doing her dishes. The joy in the wheezy voice brought a lump to her throat.

Marigold took her time as she walked up the porch steps. The railings could use a coat of rust paint. She was sure the doorbell still didn't work. Not that it mattered. The front door was always unlocked. The weathered "Angels on guard" plaque nailed above the door was meant to deter anyone with evil intentions.

Eyes closed, Marigold rested her forehead against the storm door. Once her fingers pulled the handle, there would be no turning back. The door slammed behind her as she stepped in.

"Darrell, is that you?" her grandmother asked.

Darrell was a distant relative who helped out around the house. "No. Big Momma, it's Marigold."

Her grandmother gave a shout as she hurried out of the kitchen. "You came!"

"Surprise."

Big Momma's eyes went from Marigold's face to her stomach and her smile disappeared. "I'd said there was something different about your face. How far gone are you?"

"Six months."

Big Momma's eyes flashed. "You've been pregnant for six months?"

Marigold was startled by a bang on the door. "Big Momma, I'm back."

She recognized Darrell's voice.

"Okay, dear. I'll be out," Big Momma said.

"I don't want to see him," Marigold whispered to her grandmother.

"He's not coming in. He went to buy me a cord of firewood," Big Momma whispered back.

Her grandmother's wood burning stove was big enough to warm the entire house. She gave a sigh of relief after Big Momma stepped outside. Darrell had given her a reprieve.

Restless, she walked through the house. Each time she visited, Marigold felt as if she'd found her way into a fifties time capsule. The living room walls still had light wood paneling. The kitchen's bright yellow cabinets combined with the black and white, checkered linoleum floor tiles, gave off an old-school diner vibe.

The antique, brass floor lamp had not moved from its spot. Marigold ran her fingers across the surface of the solid wood buffet next to it. Even though Big Momma had tried to buff out the dings with a walnut, the dents Ixora caused when she'd knocked over the lamp were still there.

Their big argument was caused by something insignificant. Ixora had looked her straight in the eye as she scratched her nose. "Pucker up, baby," Ixora said. "This itch tells me I'm about to kiss a fool."

She had bunched up her fingers after Ixora closed her eyes and stuck out pouty lips. "Who's the fool now?" she'd said as her sister screamed from the punch to her mouth.

Ixora had stepped back and knocked over the lamp. The noise had brought their grandmother out of her room.

"Girls, I better not see any blood on my floor," Big Momma yelled as she made her way towards the living room. "Only the good Lord knows why your parents bothered to give you such pretty names. With the way you both carry on, you should have been named Thorn and Nettle."

Marigold told in a deep breath and blew out the heavy feelings the memory brought. Thirsty, she walked over to the kitchen to pour herself a cup of Big Momma's homemade lemonade.

The almond-coloured fridge was covered with the postcards Marigold had sent from various ports. Next to them were pictures of Ixora and her family. Ixora had done what was expected of her. She'd graduated from university at the top of her business degree class, married nice guy Eli, had two adorable children and ran a bed and breakfast.

Sooner or later, Ixora would find out she was back in Mapleville. She might as well call her to break the news.

Big Momma had a calmer demeanor when she came back into the house. They sat at the kitchen table. "Does your sister know?"

"Yes. And I told her not to tell you."

"What did Logan say about all this? The boy has a lot of sense."

Sensibility was a major plus in Big Momma's books. "My life doesn't revolve around Logan's opinions," she said.

"Hmm. Is there going to be a wedding?"

Marigold shook her head.

"Why not?"

She didn't know if Logan had updated his parents. And how would she explain surrogacy to her old school grandmother? Better to go with the good old scarlet letter label. "He's married."

Big Momma closed her eyes. "Marigold Tracey Shadd."

The last time she'd heard Big Momma say her name that way was when she had called from New York to let her grandmother know she and Logan were about to join their first vessel.

"It wasn't planned," she said.

Big Momma pulled herself up from the table. "I need to go to talk to my Jesus."

Marigold rested her head on the table after her grandmother left. "You told me to come home," she said to the empty room.

When you go through deep waters, I will be with you.

CHAPTER THIRTEEN

With a large cup of coffee in her hands, Big Momma was seated at the kitchen table when Marigold woke up. Hunger pangs had forced her out of bed.

"Good morning, Big Momma."

Her grandmother gave her a faint smile. "Good morning, child."

Relieved, she poured herself some milk and cereal. After their conversation, her grandmother had spent the rest of the day in her room.

Marigold sat at the table with her heaping bowl.

"How are you feeling?" Big Momma asked.

"I'm fine."

"If you had told me you were pregnant, I would have come to Toronto," Big Momma said in a sad voice.

"There is something else I should tell you," she said.

"What is it?"

"The baby has Down Syndrome."

Big Momma closed her eyes. When she opened them, they glistened from unshed tears. "All children are gifts from God."

A gift. Before she left Toronto, she had gone to an ultrasound clinic where she could pay to find out the sex of the baby. "I'm having a boy," she said.

Big Momma gave her a shaky smile. "We need more boys in this family."

Marigold stared into her cereal bowl. The decision not to terminate the pregnancy was easy. But she doubted her ability to provide the baby with a stable home. If she gave him up for adoption, he would be placed with a loving family. They would give him a better future than the one she could provide. "I don't know if I can keep him," she said.

"What do you mean?"

"I've been thinking of giving him up for adoption."

"Marigold."

"Big Momma, you know me. Before all this happened, the plan was to go back to sea. If I keep him, he's going to need some sort of support for the rest of his life. That's a major commitment."

"Do you love this child?"

Marigold swallowed hard. Every time she felt him move, it brought her joy. She was still amazed by the way he seemed to respond to her massages, to her voice. As she read her week-by-week pregnancy updates, she was filled with pride about how much he'd grown, by the things he could do. "Yes."

"Marigold, love is a commitment."

She hung her head. "I always seem to disappoint you."

Big Momma put a finger under her chin and lifted her head. "That's not true. As long as your actions please the Lord, that's what really matters."

"I know the Lord who gave this child to us has a plan for his life, for your life. Yes, he has an extra chromosome. Still, that's just a part of a whole. I know there'll be extra challenges. But as surely as the Lord lives, there will be extra joy for the journey."

The following weekend, the Yarn Artists of Mapleville held their monthly meeting at Big Momma's home. Marigold yawned as she switched on Big Momma's forty-two-cup coffee urn. They'd spent all morning baking blueberry pies and coffee cakes. The frozen fruit came from her grandmother's farm.

Big Momma came back into the kitchen. "Are you going to join us?"

"I think it's best if I stay in the bedroom while they're here," she said.

"You can't hide for the rest of your life. Hold on. I'll be back."

Marigold stood in the doorway and listened to her grandmother's speech.

"Ladies and gentleman, I have something to say. You all know I don't like gossip so I'm going to answer some questions you haven't asked. My oldest granddaughter is here."

"The one living in Toronto?" Marigold heard someone ask.

"Yes. She's pregnant, not married, and there's no planned shotgun wedding. Any questions?"

The room fell silent. "Good. We can now get on with the rest of the evening," Big Momma said.

Marigold allowed herself to be led into the room. After Big Momma had introduced her to the new members, Marigold sat in the empty chair tucked away in the corner. After a couple of furtive glances, they seemed to have forgotten she was there.

"How did your surgery go?" The lady who had introduced herself as Ms. Scarlett with two t's asked Mrs. Howard.

Mr. Henry, the only man in the room, placed a hand on Mrs. Howard's arm. "Darling, you have to tell the ladies what you told me," he said.

Mrs. Howard placed her coffee mug on the table beside her. "Before they wheeled me into the operating room, I'd told Henry I was either going to wake up to see his face or wake up in paradise."

"And I'd told her she wasn't leaving me," Mr. Henry said.

Mrs. Howard gave him a dazzling smile before she continued with her story. "You can just imagine how I felt when I woke up after surgery and found myself alone in this really dark room. We all know heaven's a beautiful, bright place. And I sure didn't feel any flames."

"That must have been scary," Mrs. Scarlett said.

Mrs. Howard held a hand to her chest. "I was like, goodness gracious, the Catholics were right. There is purgatory."

"Oh, Henry. You're going to have your hands full with this one," Big Momma said with a laugh.

He gave Mrs. Howard an indulgent smile. "I wouldn't have it any other way."

"How are the wedding plans going?" Mrs. Scarlett asked.

Mrs. Howard sighed. "The children are making too much fuss about it. I wish we could elope."

"Marigold's a certified travel agent," Big Momma said with pride in her voice. "She can help you plan a trip."

Mrs. Howard's eyes lit up as she turned towards Marigold. "I've always wanted to go to Bangkok to ride an elephant," she said.

"Jean, have you lost your yarn pulling mind?" Big Momma asked.

Marigold smiled at Mrs. Howard. If she looked as spry as Mrs. Howard did at seventy plus, she too would jump on an elephant. "We have lots of seniors going on tours."

Big Momma pursed her lips. "Child, don't encourage her."

"She's a potential client, and the customer's always right."

Mrs. Howard guffawed. "Dear, you're hired."

Marigold kept a straight face. "Yes, ma'am."

The rest of the evening was spent debating the best kind of trip for someone who had just recovered from hip replacement surgery.

By the time Big Momma kicked out the group, in her gentle but firm way, Marigold was ready for bed. Her grandmother said they could leave the mess until the following morning. Marigold refused. She didn't put it past the woman to sneak out of her bedroom at night to wash the dishes.

As Big Momma placed the dishes back in their spot, Marigold's mind went back to Mrs. Howard and her Mr. Henry. What were the odds of finding love at their age? "Big Momma, do you get lonely?"

"No. I have lots of good people in my life."

"I mean lonely for someone like Mr. Henry."

Big Momma shook her head. "Just for your grandfather. Why are you asking?"

"I was thinking about Mrs. Howard and Mr. Henry."

Big Momma gave her a half-smile. "Those two are special." She pulled a chair from the kitchen table. "Sit. There is something else I've been meaning to talk to you about."

Marigold sat on the pulled out chair.

"You know the story of how your grandfather and I met," Big Momma said.

Marigold nodded. October 1946, Theodore Henson, an African American soldier living in Stillwater, Oklahoma, had visited his Detroit cousins. They took him to the Shubert Lafayette Theatre to see the "BAL NEGRE" dance revue. That same night, Big Momma and her friends had crossed the border to see the show. They met and fell in love. Papa later moved to Canada just to marry her.

"Your grandfather was in the 179th Infantry Regiment. The regiment's motto is, *In Omina Paratus.* In all things be prepared. He was prepared to die in battle. Nothing had prepared him for the loss of your mother. It broke him."

Marigold agreed. They'd lost her grandfather within that horrible year.

Big Momma sighed. "Until that year, I was the bubbly church lady who knew just enough Scripture to sound authentic, who volunteered for everything, took in stray people and animals just because it was what a good Christian woman should do. It was during that year that I truly understood what it takes to make the bold declaration that Christ is my solid rock and on Him alone will I stand.

"While your happiness here on earth is important to me, nothing would bring me greater joy than to know that when I go home to meet Jesus, I'll see you again. I'm prepared to go. I fear you're not."

She was trying to find her way back. "It's hard to do this salvation journey."

Big Momma nodded. "That's why it's called the straight and narrow path. You need Jesus to help you. No one can make the journey without His grace."

CHAPTER FOURTEEN

Marigold was awake when Big Momma walked into her bedroom after a knock. "We have ladies' Bible study. Are you coming?"

"I think it's best I stay home," she said.

"It's Wednesday afternoon. By now, everyone in Mapleville has heard a version of your unwed mother story."

Marigold pursed her lips. Was she meant to be comforted by that? "No, thank you."

Big Momma left without saying another word. Marigold was still in bed when she returned. "Child, did you leave this bed?"

"What is there to get up for?"

"If you were not pregnant, I would have left you alone to wallow for as long as you want. But, you're carrying my great-grandchild, so you need to get your butt out of bed."

Marigold scowled. "I don't want to."

Big Momma placed a hand on her hip. "Now!"

"I'm not a baby."

"Then think about the child in your stomach. The child needs food. And until he comes out, you're the mouth. If you won't listen, it's not too late to head back to Toronto. I can't stand by and watch you self-destruct."

Marigold swung her legs off the bed. "I'll find something to eat."

Later in the evening, Big Momma insisted on taking her along to Mapleville's craft store. Marigold tried to contain her impatience as Big Momma examined each ball of yarn as if she was looking for the one destined for greatness.

Big Momma picked up a ball of wool. "What do you think about this colour?"

It was a beautiful shade of teal. "I love it," she said.

Big Momma filled her shopping basket. "I'm going to make a shawl for my little boy."

When Marigold heard laughter behind her, she froze. What was Logan doing in Mapleville?

"Mrs. Henson?"

Marigold recognized the voice. She'd forgotten that Logan and his mother had identical laughs.

Big Momma turned around. "Hello Shirley."

"Good evening," Mrs. van Basten said to her grandmother.

Even though nothing on Mrs. van Basten's flushed face invited her hello, Marigold said it anyway. "Hello, Mrs. van Basten."

Mrs. van Basten's eyes swept over Marigold's stomach. "I guess we missed the wedding announcement," she said.

Marigold gave her a brilliant smile. "There was no wedding."

Mrs. van Basten's eyes widened. "Ooh."

Big Momma placed a hand on Marigold's arm. "Nice seeing you, Shirley. We still have a few more errands to run."

"Safe travels when you return to Toronto," Mrs. van Basten said to her.

"Thank you."

Marigold watched as Mrs. van Basten hurried along. Logan was going to get a phone call from his mama.

Marigold arrived at the VIA Rail Station five minutes before Ixora's train pulled in. Instead of calling her sister, she'd sent a text to let her know she was in Mapleville.

The next day, Ixora forwarded her ten-hour travel itinerary. After taking an early morning Greyhound bus from Owen Sound to Toronto, she would catch a train from Union Station to Mapleville. She was coming home for one night.

Marigold stood on the platform when the train pulled in. Ixora looked worn when she stepped out of her passenger car. *Why are you here?*

Ixora hurried towards her when their eyes met. "Hey, Mama."

Marigold took slow steps towards her. Even though she was older by eighteen months, with their similar physique and dimples on opposite cheeks, they could pass for twins.

"Hey, Sis." They exchanged a hug. "How was your journey?"

"It was a lot of sitting. How are you?"

"I'm fine."

"And Big Momma?"

"She can't wait for her baby to get home."

Ixora smiled. "We both know who her real baby is."

Baby had always been her sister's code word for irresponsible. "I guess you're here to gloat?" Marigold asked after they sat in the car.

Ixora paused in the middle of fastening her seatbelt. "Why do you always think the worst of me?"

"Just returning the favour."

Ixora rested her back against the car and closed her eyes. "Can we go for a drive down Main Street?"

"Big Momma's waiting."

"I came to see you. We might not get some alone time at the house."

After a quick Facetime call with Big Momma, Marigold drove them into town.

"The Cone 'N' Shake Shop is still open?" Ixora asked when she saw their old hangout spot.

"Yes." That year's Indian summer had stretched far into November. It was hard to imagine that there would be snow on the ground at Christmas time. "Last week the temps were in the 70s."

"Wow."

At Ixora's request, they stopped at the shop. As always, Ixora got a butterscotch shake while she got a swirl in a waffle cone.

Right across the road was the baseball diamond. They sat in the bleachers.

"I came to Mapleville to tell you that I'm sorry," Ixora said when they were done eating.

Marigold blinked. "You're sorry?"

"Yes. I've been jealous and angry with you for too many years. I felt your behavior trapped me into the responsible child role. After you left home, I stayed with Big Momma. Every holiday I came home so that she didn't have to be alone. Yet, no matter how right I acted, I couldn't gain more of her love. You couldn't do anything more shocking to lose it."

She shook her head. "Ixora, look at me. All I have is a high school diploma. I'm an unemployed, pregnant woman whose life just blew up in her face. Sister, you won."

"I didn't win. I lost you. I lost the perspective that everything I have is as a result of grace, unearned. All those times Big Momma prayed for you, called to tell me that she'd received one of your postcards, I should have rejoiced. Sis, I've been selfish, too."

"Why did they have to leave us? Everything changed after that."

"I don't think they wanted to," Ixora said.

Marigold had begged to go with them. Her mother had insisted on her staying behind to help Big Momma on the farm. That was what had led to their fight.

The last words she said to their mom was, "I hate you and don't bother coming back." And they never did. Pain shivers went through her body. "You can't understand."

"I know someone who does. He's the one who holds me up."

She knew Ixora was referring to Jesus. "We've been talking."

"And?"

She was reading her Bible again. "I'm struggling."

"Something tells me that as long as you keep thinking that you can do this all on your own, the peace you're looking for isn't going to come."

It was pretty much what their grandmother had said.

Ixora's arm went around her. "I love you. I always will."

She settled against her sister's shoulder. "This life isn't fair."

"No, it isn't."

When Ixora began singing one of her church songs, Marigold almost expected to look over her shoulder and see a choir in black robes and gold stoles standing on the bleachers. "Ixora, we're outside."

Her sister smiled as her soprano voice soared. As Marigold focused on the words, she began to cry. Ixora stretched her arm across Marigold's shoulders and pulled her close. "The battle is not yours, Sis. This is the time to open your heart and be vulnerable."

Being vulnerable scared her. "It's been so long. What do I say?"

"Whatever comes to your spirit," Ixora said.

Marigold took a deep breath before she closed her eyes. "I accept. I accept that my abilities are limited. I need You. Please, help me."

Call on me in the day of trouble; I will deliver you, and you will honor me.

CHAPTER FIFTEEN

After dropping off Ixora at the train station, Marigold came home and took a long nap. It had been an emotional visit. She woke up and found her grandmother in the living room. "I'm going for a drive."

"I should come with you," Big Momma said as she stood up from her knitting chair.

For the first thirteen years of her life, they had also lived in cities near the water: Halifax, Edmonton, Victoria. Her father's executive job at hydro companies took them across the country.

Marigold shook her head. "I'm just going to the beach."

Big Momma looked undecided. "In your condition, you shouldn't be far from help."

"I'll have my phone on me."

"Don't be long."

"I won't. See you later."

Marigold gave a gentle sigh when she stepped down from the porch. They still had weather. She slid back her chair after sitting behind the wheel. Her pointed stomach forced her to reach for the steering wheel.

At the beach, she parked her car in the designated area and took careful steps down the winding path which led to the water. Big Momma would tie her to the bed if she came back home with any injury.

After Marigold had managed to lower herself onto a large piece of driftwood, she realized that pulling herself up wasn't going to be an easy task. There was nothing to hold on to.

She rubbed a sore spot near her ribs. Even though the floppy sun hat gave a lot of shade, she felt fresh air against her cheeks.

The strong winds across the lake spun the huge blades on the nearby turbines. Their blinking red lights had become a part of Mapleville's nightscape. Big Momma had told the town's residents no longer wanted the turbines in their backyards. The vibrations were affecting the water wells and causing dirty turbid water.

As she stared out at the water, Marigold wished she could dip her feet into the lake. But that would require getting up and she needed help.

When she began to fret, Marigold remembered the story of Abraham and Isaac. Back in the day, Big Momma had made her and Ixora recite Father Abraham's words. She had called them an enduring declaration of faith. *The Lord will provide*. As she repeated the words, her anxiety receded.

As she craned her head to look down the length of the beach, something in her jeans bit her. "Ouch!"

A second bite brought a rush of adrenaline. Marigold scampered to her feet. She should have known better than to sit on an old driftwood log.

In a search for the culprit, her fingers pushed aside the elastic waistband. As she stared at the insect, an unexplainable joy bubbled inside her. Father Abraham had received a ram. It looked like she'd been sent a beetle. When Big Momma had said, "Sometimes help comes in unexpected forms," she was right.

After she dipped her feet in the cool water, she decided to head back home. She was a safe distance away when she noticed the man standing next to her vehicle. Her steps faltered after a second look. It was Logan. He had lost a lot of weight.

His expression was somber as he watched her approach him. Marigold was surprised by how calm she felt. Regardless of what Logan had to say, *The Lord will provide*. She stopped a few feet away from him.

"You look different," Logan said as if they were just picking up an abandoned conversation.

"Are you having a Captain Obvious moment?"

"I meant your countenance." Logan cleared his throat. "Your grandmother told me you were here."

Marigold swallowed the lump in her throat. The week after they'd left high school, it was at this beach that Logan had told her about the cruise ship job opportunity he'd come across on the Internet. "What are you doing here?"

"I came to say I'm sorry."

"You already told me that," she said.

He glanced at her stomach. "I've always prided myself on being a standup guy. But when it mattered most I failed to stand up for my child. I know we signed away our rights, but I want to stay involved in his life. On your terms."

Before she'd given her life back to Jesus, the words would have satisfied her vindictive side. Instead, they'd brought her joy. This child deserved to have his father in his life. It wasn't about her hurt feelings.

The wedding band on Logan's finger reminded her of Alena. "Does your wife know you're here?"

Logan nodded. "Yes. She's still struggling. We're getting help."

Marigold took a deep breath. "I'm going to stay in Mapleville for a while. The baby and I will keep Big Momma's company."

Logan didn't look surprised. "That would be good for everyone."

"When it's close to delivery time, I'll let you know so that you and Alena, if she wants to be there, can be at the hospital."

"Have you thought of a name for the child?"

Marigold nodded. She'd picked Asher. Her father's name. "Asher Logan Shadd."

Logan's eyes filled with tears. "It's a boy?"

"Yes. I'd planned to put your name on the birth certificate. When Alena's ready for her son, you can start the necessary legal process."

"I have to tell my parents."

Logan's mom would lose her mind. "What are you going to tell them?"

"Everything. Do you need me to stay for the meeting with my mom?"

The confrontation between her and Mrs. van Basten was long overdue. "I can handle it."

He gave her a skeptical look. "Are you sure?"

God would help her fight her battles. "Yes."

Logan stretched out his hand. "I'll see you soon."

Marigold stared at Logan's hand. The emotional intimacy between them had caused Alena so much pain. Sometimes, a man needed to leave his parents and friends in order to cleave to his wife. She shook it. "Say hello to Alena."

Marigold met Big Momma out on the porch swing. "Sorry, I stayed out this late."

"I knew you were with Logan. He's always kept you safe."

She sat beside her grandmother. In many ways, she had made Logan her God. He was human, too. "There are some things I need to tell you."

Big Momma nodded. "I'm listening."

When she was done with the rest of the story, Big Momma sighed. "If Logan and his wife come back for the boy, will you be able to give him up?"

Marigold sighed. "It's going to be hard, but he's not mine to keep."

Big Momma placed a hand on her cheek. "I'm so proud of you."

Marigold placed her hand on top of her grandmother's and felt the tremble that was too slight to see. "I'm sorry for all the trouble I caused you before I left."

"I should have tried harder to reach you."

Marigold remembered crying and not knowing why. There were days when all she wanted to do was sleep. The memorial service felt unreal because there were no bodies to bury. "I was too angry to care."

"Two nights before they left for their trip, your mother came to me. She was worried about you. And thought that maybe they should buy the last minute ticket their travel agent found. By the time they called back, someone else had taken it. I'm so thankful you didn't go with them."

"Ixora thought she had to be perfect to make up for my defiance."

"We should go and visit them at Christmas," Big Momma said.

Marigold nodded. "I'll talk to Eli, and we'll plan a surprise visit for Ixora and the children."

Big Momma gave a happy sigh. "God is faithful. Through the good and the bad."

CHAPTER SIXTEEN

The next day, Logan's mother made an unannounced visit. "I know I should have called," she said to Big Momma who had welcomed her into the house.

"We were expecting you," Big Momma said.

After she and Logan's mom sat in the living room, her grandmother announced that she had some things to do in the kitchen.

Mrs. van Basten's bloodshot eyes stared at her. "From the first time Logan came home and told me about you, I'd known you were going to be trouble. Logan had good grades. He could have gone on to any university. He changed his mind because of you."

Marigold folded her hands in her lap. "If he wants to, Logan can still attend university."

"Logan told us about his son. A child needs two committed parents in a stable home. How are you going to take care of this child on your own?"

"Single parents raise well-adjusted children. And I've decided to stay in Mapleville for a while," she said.

Mrs. van Basten gave her a skeptical look. "A child needs a parent who knows how to plant roots. You only came back to Canada because of Logan. He told us so. Tell me, what happens when staying in one place loses its novelty? If Logan and his wife don't want their child, his father and I do."

"I can take care of the baby," she said.

"As a surrogate mother, yes. However, I have serious doubts about your ability to be a real mother."

Marigold told herself that she had to stay focused on the emotions behind the angry words. It was pain and fear.

"I've done my research. Grandparents have rights, too. If we have to go to court, we will."

"And I have a legal document which states that Logan and Alena signed their rights away. If you want to go to court over this, I'm not going to stop you."

Mrs. van Basten's eyes filled with tears. "Why didn't you just marry him? He followed you around for ten years."

Marigold took a deep breath. She had done the following. Going to New York was Logan's idea. He didn't want to take over the pig farm from his father. Marigold had never thought she would say the words that came out of her mouth. "It wasn't God's will."

Mrs. van Basten snorted. "What do you know about God's will?"

Focused on their conversation, Marigold hadn't heard her grandmother's heavy footsteps. She walked into the room and stood in front of Logan's mom. "I didn't invite you in so you could beat my pregnant child down with your words. I think it's time for you to leave."

Logan's mother hung her head. "I'm sorry, Mrs. Henson."

Marigold stood when Logan's mom did. "Mrs. van Basten, I love Logan. I always will. When we met, I was the sullen new girl who sat alone with a hood pulled over her head. Logan said hello to me. Sat with me. Shared the tasty lunches you made. He found different ways to make me laugh. Protected me. He was that way because somebody, you, raised him right. I don't know what the future will bring, but I'll never keep your grandson away from you."

Big Momma wrapped her arm around Mrs. van Basten's shoulders as she cried. "It's okay. We have to trust that He has a plan for us all."

Alone in the house, Marigold took Big Momma's Bible and sat on the knitting chair. She adjusted the throw pillow until it cushioned her lower back. As she settled against the chair, it felt as if her grandmother's warmth radiated from the plaid fabric.

At the top of Big Momma's knitting basket was a teal shawl. Asher's shawl. Marigold held it up and saw a hanging thread. She wasn't sure why Big Momma had left it there. She took a closer look. The thread didn't take away from the shawl's beauty.

Marigold laid the shawl over her stomach. Moments later, Asher kicked. "You can feel the softness? I was going to play that Baby Mozart for you. But, I think we should do some reading from your great-grandma's Bible. She loves her Psalms."

She read the first three verses of Psalm One aloud:

Blessed is the one
who does not walk in step with the wicked
or stand in the way that sinners take
or sit in the company of mockers,
but whose delight is in the law of the Lord,
and who meditates on his law day and night
That person is like a tree planted by streams of water,
which yields its fruit in season
and whose leaf does not wither—
whatever they do prospers.

Marigold stopped to meditate on the words. She didn't know how to plant deep roots, but she was getting to know the Master Tree Planter. He would anchor them in the right spot.

"Did you hear that, Asher? If we stay plugged into Him, we're going to flourish."

Marigold gave her stomach a pat, adjusted her position in the chair, and continued to read.

-The End-

BOOK CLUB DISCUSSION QUESTIONS

1. What are some of the major themes in *Knit Together*? Were they well developed by the author?

2. What are your thoughts around surrogacy? Are there reasons why Christians should not act as surrogates?

3. How effective was the author in presenting the Christian faith in a way that is relevant to the lives of the characters?

4. What did you think of the relationship between Marigold and Logan? Did it cross any lines?

5. If you were in Alena's shoes, how would you react to the Down Syndrome diagnosis?

6. Sibling rivalry has been a hot topic since the time of Cain and Abel. What did you think of the relationship between Marigold and Ixora?

7. What did you think of Marigold's path to redemption? Was it genuine?

8. Were you disappointed in Logan for abandoning his child? What would you have liked to see happen?

9. What did you think of the relationship between Marigold and Archibong? Do they have a future?

10. Marigold's grandmother expressed some regrets about how she had handled Marigold's grief. What are the best ways to support grieving children?

11. Do you think that Marigold should give Asher to his parents if they were to return for him? Why or why not?

12. Knit Together is a redemptive story. What brings people to redemption?

EXCERPT FROM SECRET PLACES

Moni's eyes scanned the letter she had found in her work mailbox. The letter, signed by the company's human resource manager, advised her that effective from the next pay period, she had been given a very generous raise.

Instead of doing a victory fist pump, she flung the letter on her desk before covering her face. Anxiety muddled her mind and held her stomach in a vicious grip. There was no room for joy.

Moni dropped her hands. She was not being paid to focus on personal problems during company time. She switched on her computer and re-opened the document she'd been working on. She rubbed the base of her thumbs over her eyes as she wondered how she was going to meet her looming deadline. The smiles she'd been getting from management since the DressCo deal went through were sure to disappear if she messed up this assigned sales pitch.

Shoulders hunched, Moni willed herself to focus as she tried reading the document from the beginning. Despite her resolve, nothing was sinking in.

The words blurred and her mind wandered off again. Her thoughts traveled back to the first time she'd met Sam. He was twenty and she had just turned eighteen. He was a new member of their church. He and Debo were serving as members of her father's select group of armour bearers.

As a little girl, she'd thought the young men carried real armours. But their role was more like the pastor's helper. They carried her father's Bible, bottle of water and did anything else that needed to be done. Because the group of young men were frequently invited over their house for meals, she grew to know them. Her parents' undisguised acceptance of Sam and those warm childhood memories made it easy to love him. With her parents against dating just for the fun of it, Sam had been her first and last serious boyfriend.

Through their one-year courtship and twenty-year marriage, her parents had continued to be his champions. Moni imagined how shocked they would be if she told them what he wanted her to do.

Moni thought that Sam would come back to say he was mistaken. Instead, he bounced around the house looking as if he had rediscovered his life's purpose.

Yes, she struggled with staying committed to God. Still, Moni found it hard to accept that swinging was the right thing for them to do. Even if a husband and wife were in agreement about swinging, she doubted it made it right for them to commit what she'd been taught was a sin.

Her tired eyes landed on the picture frame propped up on her desk. Shekinah's round face smiled at Moni from the grade eight graduation picture. Her fingers reached out and caressed the glass.

After he'd told her about the play parties, Sam had declared that Shekinah's behavioral problems were linked to the sorry state of their marriage. Like she didn't know this already.

Things were much better than they had been in months, but Shekinah was still her father's daughter. In the event of a divorce, Shekinah may decide to live at Sam's house. He wouldn't discourage her. And if she did, Moni knew that she would lose her daughter. Sam couldn't grasp that this wasn't the time for them to be Shekinah's friend.

Contrary to what Shekinah must think when she said no to her requests, she loved her. How could she not? The thought of losing her only child had stripped ten pounds off her body in just two weeks.

Conscious of the thin walls of her office cubicle, Moni placed her hand over her mouth to muffle a cry. She didn't know what to do.

Beloved, trust Me.

Tears filled her eyes as fear's roar continued to build inside her mind.

www.ingramcontent.com/pod-product-compliance
Lightning Source LLC
Chambersburg PA
CBHW020313150626
46552CB00022B/2875